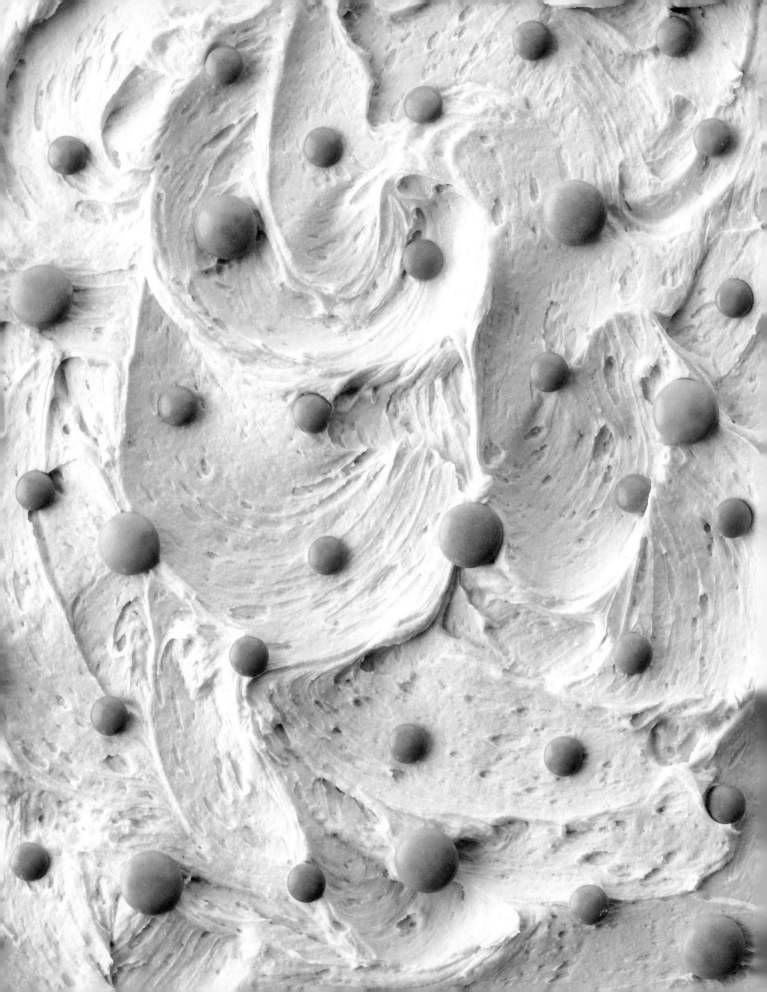

Lulu
and Harry
in

The
Best Ever
Birthday

Acknowledgements

An enormous thank you to all my family for living and breathing *The Best Ever Birthday* this year. Your patience while I hijacked family gatherings with recipe testing, cake decorating and rhyming brainstorms has meant so much. Thanks also to Sue Fichtner, who has been the most amazing support. I truly would have been lost without you.

To my fairy godmother, Jannie Brown, thank you for your unwavering friendship and encouragement, and for being my Melbourne mum. And to Olivia and Isabel Brindley, many thanks for all your brilliant ideas, which appear throughout the book.

Thank you to Adam Cremona for your cake inspirations. You are a clever socks indeed.

I'm also grateful to Deborah Kaloper and Emma Christian for your tireless efforts during our photo shoot. You are both wonderful cooks and transformed a hectic schedule into a lot of fun. Thanks also to Chris Middleton for your stunning photography.

A huge thank you to everyone at Hardie Grant. Thanks to Helen Chamberlin for another round of fine editing, and particular thanks to my wonderful publisher, Paul McNally, and editor, Lucy Heaver, for your vision, guidance and support. I feel blessed to work with such a talented publishing team.

Finally, extra special thanks to the inimitable Michelle Mackintosh, who is both a creative genius and a total treasure. It is an absolute privilege to be in partnership with you.

Published in 2012 by Hardie Grant Books
Hardie Grant Books (Australia)
Ground Floor, Building 1
658 Church Street
Richmond, Victoria 3121
www.hardiegrant.com.au

Hardie Grant Books (UK)
Dudley House, North Suite
34–35 Southampton Street
London WC2E 7HF
www.hardiegrant.co.uk

National Library of Australia Cataloguing-in-Publication Data:
Cataloguing-in-Publication data is available from the National Library of Australia.

The Best Ever Birthday
ISBN: 978 1 74270 292 6

Publishing Director: Paul McNally
Designed, illustrated and styled by Michelle Mackintosh
Edited by Helen Chamberlin and Lucy Heaver
Photographed by Chris Middleton
Food preparation by Louise Fulton Keats, Deborah Kaloper and Emma Christian
Colour reproduction by Splitting Image Colour Studio
Printed in China by 1010 Printing International Limited

Lulu and Harry in

The Best Ever Birthday

Louise Fulton Keats
Recipes inspired by Margaret Fulton
Illustrated by Michelle Mackintosh

hardie grant books
MELBOURNE · LONDON

Contents

To Harry, Finlay,
Grace & Ruby,
may we celebrate
many more
birthdays together.

Nutmeg

sous-chef
A sous-chef
is the
head chef's
assistant!

My name is Lulu and I love to cook.

I make lots of dishes from Grandma's cookbook.

My brother Harry is my helpful 'sous-chef',

And Nutmeg cleans up any mess that we've left!

Thanks to Grandma, I know all about chopping,

And how to make cakes with the best icing topping.

I can even cook meals for celebrity guests ...

Though they do make some rather demanding requests!

But I have the *most* fun when there's a birthday.

Harry helps me make ice cream and frosty sorbet.

There are jellies to set and biscuits to bake,

And, the best part of all, there's the birthday cake!

'Whose birthday is next?' I ask Grandma one day,
So she looks up her calendar right away.
'We've had Harry's and Teddy's and even mine too,
So coming up next ... look, it's yours, Lulu!'

Monday	Tuesday	Wednesday	Thursday	Friday	Saturday	Sunday
30	01	02	03	04	05	06
07	08	09	10	*Lulu's birthday* 11	12	13
14	15	16	17	18	19	20
21	22	23	24	25	26	27
28	29	30	31	01	02	03

04	05	06	07	08	09	10
11	12	13	14	15	16	17
18	19	20	21	22	23	24

Ooooh, yippee for that, I'm so excited!

I might have a party where everyone's invited.

I must call a meeting with my support team,

So we can start planning and choosing the theme!

Harry, Teddy and Nutmeg, you are ALL needed in the kitchen for an ESPECIALLY important meeting, right now!

We all sit around and brainstorm our thoughts.

'I know!' says Harry. 'Let's be astronauts!'

I like the idea of a party on Mars ...

We could have rocket fruit sticks and biscuit stars!

For Outer Space Party recipes
see pages 42–47

13

But, I also really like being a fairy.

Even Nutmeg wears wings (they just get a bit hairy).

We could make fairy cupcakes and pink jellies too!

'Harry, would you mind putting on a tutu?'

For Fairy Party recipes see pages 48–53

But Harry says, 'I want us to be dinosaurs!
I'll be Stegosaurus or T-rex with claws!'
I guess that sounds fun — although what would I bake?
Harry says, 'Nothing's better than dinosaur cake!'

For Dinosaur Party recipes see pages 54-59

Or how about a circus, with balloons and a clown?

'But there aren't any dinosaurs!' Harry says with a frown.

But we *could* serve ice creams with two or three scoops,

And even teach Nutmeg to jump through some hoops!

For Circus Party recipes
see pages 60–65

Then Teddy jumps up and starts clapping his paws:

'Let's have a teddy bears' picnic outdoors!'

I suspect he just wants us to dress up like bears.

But I *do* like those sandwiches cut into squares.

For Picnic Party recipes
see pages 66–71

Let's see — astronauts, fairies, dinosaurs with claws,

Clowns at the circus or teddies with paws.

Which one should I choose? Is there something else left?

Then Harry says, 'How about ... a party for *chefs*?'

For Chefs Party recipes
see pages 72–79

Perfect! Of course! Why didn't I think of that?

We can all have an apron, a whisk and a hat.

And I'll make a cake everyone will adore.

My friends can all try it and give it a score!

11/10

10/10

10/10

Hmmm ... I'll just need to think of the perfect cake.

Harry says, 'Choose the one that's the most *fun* to make!'

But I tell him a chef's cake must look amazing,

With several layers, decorations and glazing.

My birthday is here and everything's just right!
All my friends look like top chefs, dressed up in white.
We've done lots of cooking and won lots of prizes,
And now we're all watching my
cake as it rises.

And now the last layer ... I've got to be steady ...

And pipe on the icing ... It's almost ready ...

Add the last decorations ... Not long to go ...

My fancy chef's cake was looking so perfect,

And now it's completely and utterly WRECKED!

My party is ruined, it's my *worst* ever birthday.

My friends may as well just go home straight away.

But then I remember what Grandma likes to say:

'Do you know how to pick a top chef right away?

It's not always the fanciest, or the most swish,

It's the one who can *rescue* any dish!'

And that's when I come up with a little plan.

If a top chef could handle this, maybe *I* can ...

'Who can help me make icing? We need it *bright* green!

Let's make the best *dinosaur* you've ever seen!'

I draw up a sketch so there's not one mistake.

We can start out by icing the broken-up cake.

Then put spikes on the top and spots underneath,

And use raisins for eyes and almonds for teeth!

raisin
eyes

chocolate
spikes

spots
all over

green
icing

almond
teeth

Well, I can't say he turned out exactly as planned.

He's kind of lopsided and he can't really stand.

He's missing an eye, and his tail sort of split.

But ... we're laughing so much,
we don't care one bit!

So, as it turns out, Harry was right.

Even top chefs, all dressed up in white,

Don't need fancy cakes with a perfect score ...

They just like having fun — and some squashed dinosaur!

Recipes

Basic butter cake

125 g butter, softened
¾ cup caster sugar
½ teaspoon vanilla extract

2 eggs
1 ½ cups self-raising flour, sifted
½ cup milk

Preheat the oven to 170°C (150°C fan). Grease and line a 20 cm round cake tin (or line three 6-hole (80 ml) cupcake tins with paper or silicone cases).

Using an electric mixer, beat the butter, sugar and vanilla until pale and fluffy. Add the eggs, one at a time, and beat until well combined. Using a spoon or spatula, fold in the flour and milk until just combined.

Transfer the mixture to the tin/s and spread evenly. Bake for 45–50 minutes (20–25 minutes, if making cupcakes) or until a skewer inserted into the centre comes out clean. Leave in the tin/s for 10 minutes before transferring to a wire rack to cool.

Basic chocolate cake: to make a chocolate version of this cake, replace ¼ cup flour with ¼ cup cocoa powder.

makes 1 cake or 18 cupcakes

Butter cream icing

125 g butter, softened
1 ½ cups icing sugar, sifted

1–2 tablespoons milk

Using an electric mixer, beat the butter until very pale. Add the icing sugar and 1 tablespoon of the milk and beat until light and fluffy. Add the remaining milk if needed, for desired consistency.

Chocolate icing: to make chocolate icing, add ⅓ cup cocoa to the icing sugar.

Outer Space Party

Rocket fruit sticks

60 large cubes of assorted
fruit (choose from
pineapple, melon,
mango, banana)

20 strawberries, hulled
20 wooden icy pole sticks
or skewers
fruit yoghurt, to serve

Thread 3 pieces of fruit onto each icy pole stick or skewer,
followed by 1 strawberry — this will be the top of the
rocket. If using banana, brush a little lemon juice
over each piece to stop it from browning.

Serve with yoghurt on the
side for dipping.

makes 20

Rainbow star biscuits

100 g butter, softened
½ cup icing sugar
1 egg

1 ½ cups plain flour
25 sugar-free fruit drops
25 Mini M&Ms

Using an electric mixer, beat the butter and icing sugar until pale and fluffy. Add the egg and beat until well combined. Using a spoon or spatula, fold in the flour until a smooth dough forms. Turn the dough onto a lightly-floured surface and shape into a disc (about 12 cm diameter). Cover with plastic wrap and refrigerate for 1 hour or until firm.

Preheat the oven to 180°C (160°C fan). Line 2 large baking trays with baking paper.

Take the dough from the refrigerator and roll out between two pieces of baking paper to 5-6 mm thickness. Using a 7 cm star cutter, cut stars from the dough, and place onto the baking trays. Using a 4 cm star cutter, cut small stars out of the centre of each large star and place these on the baking trays. Repeat with the remaining dough, re-rolling any dough scraps.

Place 1 fruit drop in the centre of each large star and 1 Mini M&M in the centre of each small star. Bake, one tray at a time, for 8 minutes or until the biscuits are golden. Leave the biscuits on the trays until cool.

makes about 50 (25 small, 25 large)

If the dough becomes too soft to handle, place it back in the refrigerator (or briefly in the freezer) until firm.

Chocolate meteoroids

100 g stoned dates

170 g raisins or sultanas

½ cup almond meal

2 tablespoons cocoa
powder

2 teaspoons fresh orange
juice

½ cup desiccated coconut,
plus an extra ⅓ cup for
coating

Place the dates and raisins
in the small bowl of a food processor
and blend until finely chopped.
Add 2 tablespoons of boiling water and
leave to soak for 1 minute.

Add the almond meal, cocoa powder, orange juice
and desiccated coconut, and blend until
the mixture forms a smooth paste.

Spread the extra desiccated coconut onto a flat
surface. Using your hands, separate the mixture
into small balls and roll in the coconut.
Store in an airtight container in the
refrigerator for up to 1 week.

makes about 35

Galaxy cake

2 × quantities basic butter cake
    (see page 41) or 2 × 440 g
    packet butter cake mix
blue and yellow food colouring
    (natural, if available)

400 g ready-to-roll white icing
10 pieces white florist's wire, cut in half
1 × quantity butter cream icing
    (see page 41)
silver cachous, to decorate

Preheat the oven to 170°C (150°C fan). Grease and line a deep 22 cm round cake tin.

Make the butter cake mixture and spread into the prepared tin. Bake for about 1 hour or until a skewer inserted into the centre comes out clean. Leave in the tin for 10 minutes before transferring to a wire rack to cool.

Knead the white icing until soft. Divide into four portions (three of equal size and one smaller for the yellow moon). Leave one portion white and tint the remaining portions different colours — light blue, dark blue and yellow for the smaller portion — by kneading through the food colouring, starting with a few drops and adding more as needed.

Roll out half of each icing portion, apart from the yellow, on a surface lightly dusted with icing sugar or cornflour (or between 2 sheets of baking paper) to 5 mm thickness. Cut out star shapes with a star cutter and thread onto the florist's wires by dipping the ends of the wires into water and inserting half way into the stars. Set aside on plastic wrap and allow to dry completely.

Meanwhile, trim the domed top off the cooled cake and turn cut-side down onto a cake board or plate. Make the butter cream icing and add a few drops of blue food colouring, adding more as needed until the desired colour is reached. Spread the icing over the entire cake, making it as smooth as possible.

Roll out the yellow icing to 2–3 mm thickness. Using an 8 cm round cutter make a crescent moon shape and place on top of the cake. Roll out the remaining icing portions to 2–3 mm thickness, and use small and large star cutters to cut out shapes and arrange on the cake as desired.

Using the picture as a guide, place silver cachous on the cake top and sides. Slightly bend the wires on the wired stars and place in the cake before serving.

Natural food colouring is available from some major supermarkets and specialty food stores.

If you like rockets, you can put one like me on your cake instead of the moon!

Rocket variation: colour 100 g ready-to-roll white icing with red food colouring, roll to 2–3 mm thickness and, using the picture as a guide, cut out rocket shapes with a sharp knife. Instead of making a moon, use the yellow icing to make the yellow elements of the rocket.

Freezing the cake for a couple of hours or refrigerating it overnight will make it easier to apply the butter cream icing.

Fairy Party

Pink fairy cupcakes

60 g butter, softened

⅓ cup caster sugar

¼ teaspoon vanilla extract

1 egg

¾ cup self-raising flour, sifted

¼ cup milk

½ teaspoon natural pink
food colouring

½ cup single pouring cream,
whipped

⅓ cup strawberry (or any red) jam

sifted icing sugar for dusting

Preheat the oven to 170°C (150°C fan). Line two 12-hole (20 ml)
mini cupcake tins with paper or silicone cases.

Using an electric mixer, beat the butter, sugar and vanilla until pale and
fluffy. Add the egg and beat until well combined. Using a spoon or spatula,
fold in the flour, milk and food colouring until just combined.

Transfer the mixture to the cases and spread evenly. Bake for about
20 minutes or until a skewer inserted into the centre comes out clean.
Leave in the tins for 5 minutes before transferring to a wire rack to cool.

To fill the fairy cakes, cut a shallow round from the top of each cupcake
with a sharp pointed knife. Fill each cupcake with cream and jam, then
replace the tops. Dust with icing sugar and serve.

makes 24

Raspberry jellies

2 × punnets raspberries

2 × 85 g packets raspberry
jelly crystals

2 cups boiling water

1 ¾ cups cold water

½ cup single pouring cream,
whipped

Divide 1 punnet of the raspberries between
14 watertight cupcake cases.

Combine the jelly crystals and the boiling water in a medium jug,
stirring until the crystals dissolve. Stir in the cold water.
Pour the liquid evenly over the raspberries and refrigerate for
3–4 hours or until the jelly sets.

Top each jelly with a spoonful of whipped cream
and the remaining raspberries.

makes 14

Chocolate-dipped strawberries

24 large strawberries,
washed and dried

12 wooden icy pole sticks

150 g milk, dark or white
chocolate (or use a
mixture of all three)

Line a large baking tray with baking paper. Using scissors, cut the icy pole sticks in half crossways and push 1 strawberry onto each icy pole stick.

Break the chocolate into small, even pieces and place in a heatproof bowl. Fill a small saucepan with one-third water, bring to the boil, then reduce the heat to low. Put the heatproof bowl on top of the saucepan (it shouldn't be touching the water) and, using a metal or silicone spoon, stir the chocolate until it is melted and smooth.

Dip the strawberries into the chocolate. Place onto the baking tray and refrigerate for about 2 hours, until set.

Tip: you can use bananas instead of strawberries. After dipping them in chocolate, put them in the freezer until partially frozen. Yummy!

makes 24

Fairy tutu pavlovas

4 egg whites
1 cup caster sugar
natural pink food colouring

1 cup single pouring cream, whipped
6 strawberries, hulled and sliced
rose Persian fairy floss

Preheat the oven to 120°C (100°C fan). Line 2 large baking trays with baking paper. Draw 6 circles 7 cm in diameter (using a 7 cm round cutter is a good guide) on each sheet of baking paper, a few centimetres apart.

Using an electric mixer, beat the egg whites until soft peaks form. Gradually beat in the sugar, one spoonful at a time, until the mixture is thick and glossy. Beat in the food colouring, starting with a few drops, until the desired colour is reached.

Divide the meringue mixture between the circles on the baking paper and use a palette knife to spread it out onto the rounds. Make a slight hollow in the centre of each.

Bake for 90 minutes. Turn off the oven and leave the meringues inside to cool completely.

Once cool, remove the meringues from the oven, and top with the cream, strawberries and fairy floss.

makes 12

Persian fairy floss is available from gourmet food stores.

Dinosaur Party

Green dinosaur dip

300 g frozen peas
400 g can chickpeas,
　rinsed and drained
1 garlic clove, crushed
½ teaspoon ground cumin

juice of 1 lemon
⅓ cup extra-virgin olive oil
1 tablespoon tahini paste
toast, cut out with dinosaur-
　shaped cutter, to serve

Cook the frozen peas according to packet instructions,
until tender. Refresh with cold water and drain.

Add the peas and the remaining ingredients, except the toast,
to a food processor and blend until smooth.

Transfer the dip to a bowl and serve with the
dinosaur toasts.

makes 2 ½ cups

Jurassic pies

1 tablespoon olive oil

1 medium brown onion, finely chopped

400 g minced beef

2 tablespoons tomato paste

2 tablespoons Worcestershire sauce

¾ cup beef stock

5 sheets ready-rolled shortcrust pastry

1 egg, lightly beaten

Heat the oil in a large frying pan. Add the onion and sauté for 5 minutes or until soft. Add the beef and cook, stirring for 6–8 minutes, until browned. Add the tomato paste, Worcestershire sauce and stock, and bring to the boil, stirring. Reduce the heat and simmer, uncovered, for 10 minutes or until thickened. Set aside to cool completely.

Preheat the oven to 200°C (180°C fan). Lay out the pastry on a chopping board. Cut out 36 rounds with a 6.5 cm round cutter. Gently push the rounds into three 12-hole mini (30 ml) non-stick flat-based patty pan tins.

Divide the beef mixture between the pastry cases. Using a 5.5 cm round cutter, cut 36 rounds from the remaining pastry. Use a dinosaur-shaped cutter to cut out shapes from the centres of these rounds and then place the rounds on top of the pies. Brush each top with egg.

Bake in the oven for about 15 minutes or until golden.

makes 36

You can cook the dinosaur cut-out shapes too!

Sparkly green frappé

4 kiwi fruits, skins removed
  and chopped
small handful fresh mint leaves

2 cups apple juice
2 cups lemonade or
  sparkling mineral water

Place all the ingredients in a blender and
process until smooth and frothy.

makes 2 ½ cups

Dinosaur cake

3 × quantities basic butter cake
(see page 41) or 3 × 440 g
packet butter cake mix
2 × quantities butter cream icing
(see page 41)
green food colouring (natural)
Toblerone chocolate bar,
to decorate

green Smarties, Mini M&Ms
and Skittles, to decorate
1 raisin
1 white chocolate button
5 cm × 2 mm liquorice strap
1 red Mini M&M
1 brown Mini M&M
flaked almonds, to decorate

Preheat the oven to 170°C (150°C fan). Grease and line a 22 cm × 30 cm rectangular tin.

Make the butter cake mixture and spread evenly into the prepared tin. Bake for about 1 hour or until a skewer inserted into the centre comes out clean. Leave the cake in the tin for 10 minutes before transferring to a wire rack to cool.

Make the butter cream icing and add a few drops of green food colouring, adding more as needed until the desired colour is reached. Using the dinosaur template on pages 80–81, trace the shape onto baking paper, then place on top of the cake and cut out the dinosaur shape with a small sharp knife. Transfer to a cake board or large platter. Secure the tail-piece to the body with a little butter cream icing. Spread the remaining icing over the entire cake, making it as smooth as possible.

Using the picture as a guide, decorate the dinosaur's back with Toblerone pieces and its body with the green lollies. Make the face by securing the raisin to the chocolate button with a little butter cream, then positioning it on the head. Make the mouth with the liquorice strap and red Mini M&M. Position the remaining brown Mini M&M as the dinosaur's nose. Trim the almonds to size with a small knife and use as teeth.

Cauliflower 'popcorn'

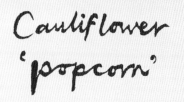

800 g cauliflower, cut into small florets

3 tablespoons olive oil

⅔ cup freshly grated parmesan cheese

Preheat the oven to 180°C (160°C fan). In a large bowl, toss the cauliflower with the olive oil. Transfer to a large baking tray and roast in the oven for 25–30 minutes or until tender and golden brown.

Tip the cauliflower into a large bowl, sprinkle over the grated parmesan and toss thoroughly. Serve warm in paper cups, like popcorn.

Pinwheel tuna sandwiches

180 g can tuna, drained
2 spring onions, ends
    trimmed and finely sliced

¼ cup finely grated carrot
250 g spreadable cream cheese
15 slices bread, crusts removed

In a bowl mix together the tuna, spring onion, carrot and cream cheese until well combined, breaking up any chunks of tuna. Place the bread on a chopping board and flatten each slice with a rolling pin (or you can use the palm of your hand), until they are nice and thin. Top each slice with a heaped tablespoon of tuna mixture and spread to the edges. Roll up tightly.

Wrap the rolled bread slices tightly with plastic wrap, twist the ends to secure and refrigerate until needed (or you can use straight away without refrigerating). Remove from the refrigerator and slice each roll into 4 or 5 pieces, about 2 cm wide.

makes 60–75

Choc-top ice creams

24 mini ice cream cones
1 litre ice cream (vanilla or
 another flavour of your choice)
sprinkles or small silver cachous,
 to decorate

Chocolate sauce
200 g dark chocolate, chopped
25 g copha, chopped

Line a large baking tray with baking paper. Top each cone with 1 scoop of
ice cream and place on the tray. Put in the freezer for 1 hour or
until very firm.

Remove the cones from the freezer and dip each into the chocolate sauce
(see below) to coat the ice cream. Sprinkle over the decorations and freeze
for a further 5–10 minutes or until the chocolate has set.

Chocolate sauce: place the chocolate and copha in a microwave-safe bowl.
Microwave, uncovered, on medium power for 3 minutes or until melted,
stirring occasionally with a metal spoon. Stir until well combined and set
aside for 5 minutes.

makes 24

circus cupcakes

1 × quantity basic butter
cake (see page 41)

1 × quantity butter cream
icing (see page 41)

Make the cupcakes according to the basic butter cake
recipe and set aside to cool.

Make the butter cream icing and spread over the
cooled cupcakes. Decorate with the circus cupcake
toppings on the opposite page.

makes 18

Popcorn buckets

pre-popped popcorn

Top each cupcake with popcorn.

Note: popcorn cupcakes should not be served to children under 5 years of age as popcorn can be a choking hazard.

decorates 6 cupcakes

Clown faces

2 red sour straps

2 multi-coloured sour straps

2 red jelly snakes

chocolate writing icing

6 Jaffas

Cut the red sour straps into 6 smiley mouths and the multi-coloured sour straps into triangles for the clown's hat. Using scissors, snip the snakes into thin slivers for the clown's hair. Decorate the cupcakes as shown, using the writing icing to draw eyes and Jaffas for the nose.

decorates 6 cupcakes

Big Top circus tents

6 red sour straps

6 flag toppers

Using the picture as a guide, cut the red sour straps into triangles and place on top of the cupcakes. Top each cupcake with a flag topper.

decorates 6 cupcakes

Picnic
Party

Chicken Waldorf sandwiches

200 g cooked free-range chicken, chopped
1 small apple, cored and coarsely chopped
⅓ cup walnuts
1 celery stalk, ends trimmed and sliced
⅔ cup mayonnaise
20 slices thin sandwich bread

Place the chicken, apple, walnuts, celery and mayonnaise in a food processor and blend until almost smooth (it's nice to leave a little bit of crunchy texture).

Place 10 of the bread slices on a chopping board and top with the chicken mixture and the remaining bread.

Trim the crusts from the sandwiches and cut into quarters to serve, or cut out with flower-shaped cutters.

makes 40 sandwich squares

If you have guests with nut allergies, you can replace the walnuts with an extra celery stalk.

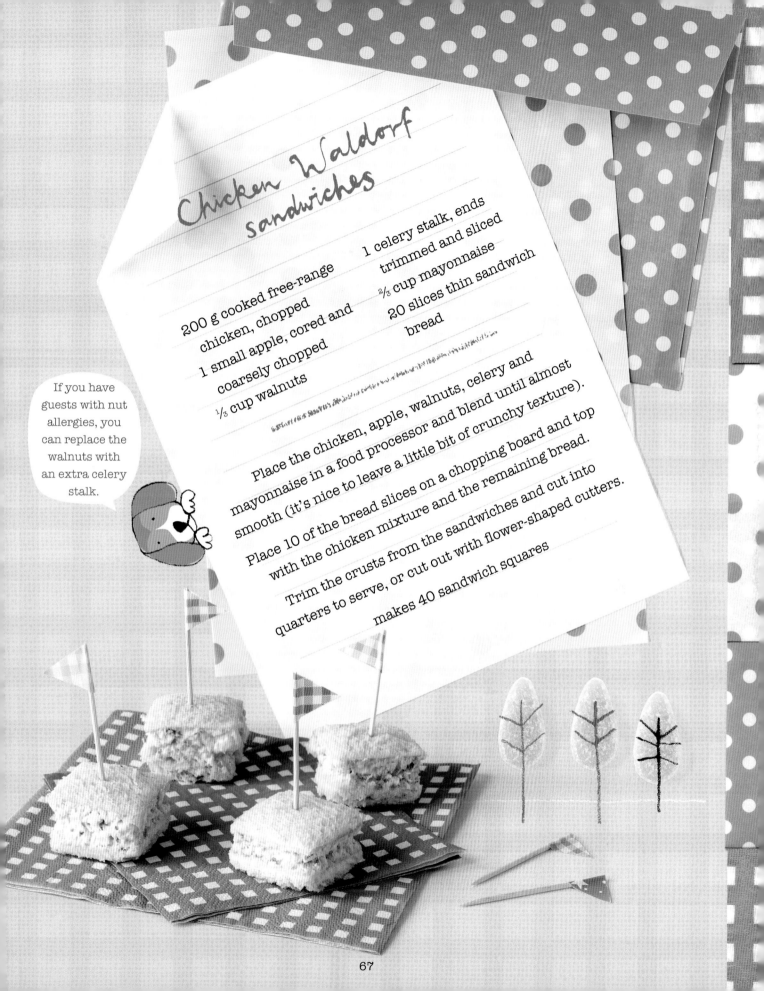

Sausage rolls

450 g minced beef

1 cup finely grated carrot

½ cup finely grated zucchini

2 spring onions, halved lengthways
and finely sliced

2 tablespoons finely chopped
flat-leaf parsley

1 teaspoon thyme leaves

2 tablespoons tomato sauce

2 sheets frozen puff pastry
(24 cm × 24 cm), just thawed

1 egg, lightly beaten

2 tablespoons sesame seeds

Preheat the oven to 200°C (180°C fan). Line a large baking tray
with baking paper.

Put the minced beef in a large bowl. Using your hands, squeeze the grated
carrot and zucchini to remove any excess moisture before adding to the
mince. Mix together with the spring onion, herbs and tomato sauce until
well combined.

Cut each pastry sheet in half. Place the 4 pieces of pastry on a chopping
board and place a quarter of the mixture in the centre of each, running
lengthways. Lightly brush the pastry edges with water. Fold the pastry
over the mince to form a roll and press the edges together. Turn the
pastry over so the 'seam' side is facing down.

Brush each roll with beaten egg, sprinkle with sesame seeds
and cut into 6 pieces. Place on the baking tray and bake
for 25 minutes or until the pastry is golden.

makes 24 mini rolls

You can freeze
the sausage rolls
cooked or uncooked.
If you've frozen them
uncooked, there is no
need to defrost
them — just bake
them for an extra
10–15 minutes.

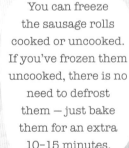

Gingerbread bears

125 g butter, softened
½ cup brown sugar
⅔ cup golden syrup
2 ½ cups plain flour
2 teaspoons ground ginger
2 teaspoons mixed spice
1 teaspoon bicarbonate of soda
Smarties or currants, to decorate

If the dough becomes too soft to handle, place it back in the refrigerator (or briefly in the freezer) until firm.

Using an electric mixer, beat the butter and sugar until pale and fluffy. Beat in the golden syrup and, using a spoon or spatula, fold in the flour, ginger, mixed spice and bicarbonate of soda until a smooth dough forms. Divide the mixture in half and form each into a disc shape. Cover in plastic wrap and refrigerate for 2–3 hours until firm.

Preheat the oven to 180°C (160°C fan). Line 2 large baking trays with baking paper.

Take 1 dough disc from the refrigerator and roll it out between 2 sheets of baking paper to 5 mm thickness. Cut shapes using a teddy bear cutter, re-rolling any dough scraps. Decorate each bear with Smarties or currants. Place the bears on the baking trays and bake for 8–10 minutes until golden (the biscuits will still be soft when taken from the oven, but will firm while cooling). Meanwhile, repeat the process with the second dough disc, baking the bears in batches if necessary. Transfer to a wire rack to cool.

makes 24

Picnic cupcakes

1 × quantity basic
  butter cake (see page 41)
1 × quantity butter
  cream icing (see page 41)
400 g ready-to-roll
  white icing

brown and red food
  colouring (natural,
  if available)
black edible ink pen
3 lolly mint leaves,
  cut into quarters

If you prefer chocolate
cupcakes, you can make the
chocolate version of the basic
butter cake instead. Yum!

Make the cupcakes according to
the basic butter cake recipe and set aside to cool.
If the tops have domed, trim them down to be level
with the cupcake cases. Make the butter cream
icing and spread over the cooled cupcakes.

Knead the white icing until soft. Tint 200 g
of the white icing with brown food colouring
by kneading it through, starting with a few
drops and adding more as needed. Tint 150 g
of the white icing with red food colouring,
wrap in plastic wrap to prevent drying
and set aside.

Black edible ink pens are available from cake decorating suppliers and some specialty food stores.

To make the teddy cupcakes, roll out the brown icing on a surface lightly dusted with icing sugar or cornflour (or between 2 sheets of baking paper) to 2–3 mm thickness. Cut out 9 larger circles using a 3.5 cm round cutter and 18 smaller circles using a 1.5 cm round cutter, keeping the left-over brown icing to make apple stalks (see below). Set aside the circles on plastic wrap. Roll out the white icing to 2–3 mm thickness and cut out 9 circles with the 1.5 cm round cutter. Place the white circles on the larger brown circles and place 2 small brown circles at the top for ears. Roll small balls of white icing and position on the ears, and draw on the eyes, nose and mouth using the black edible ink pen.

To make the apple cupcakes, use the remaining brown icing to roll 9 thin 1 cm stalks, discarding any excess. Set aside on plastic wrap. Roll out the red icing on a surface lightly dusted with icing sugar or cornflour (or between 2 sheets of baking paper) to 2–3 mm thickness. Using a 4 cm apple-shaped cutter, cut out 9 apple shapes.

Place the finished teddy bear faces and apple shapes on the iced cupcakes, attaching the brown icing stalks and quartered mint leaves to each apple.

makes 18

Fancy Chefs Party

Ham and cheese spirals

2 sheets frozen puff pastry
(24 cm × 24 cm), just thawed
125 g spreadable cream cheese
200 g thinly sliced free-range ham

½ cup grated parmesan cheese
½ cup grated cheddar cheese
1 egg, lightly beaten

Preheat the oven to 200°C (180°C fan). Line a large baking tray
with baking paper.

Place the pastry sheets on a large chopping board. Spread with
cream cheese and top with the ham and grated cheeses. Roll up
each sheet tightly, pressing the edges together. Cut each sheet into
2 cm-wide spirals and place on the baking tray. Brush the sides
and tops with egg and bake for 12 minutes, or until golden brown.
Transfer to a wire rack to cool.

makes 24

At your Fancy Chefs
party, all your friends
can join in with the
cooking!

Rice paper rolls

50 g rice vermicelli
2 tablespoons lemon juice
1 tablespoon fish sauce
1 tablespoon soy sauce or tamari
2 teaspoons brown sugar
250 g cooked free-range chicken,
    finely shredded
1 carrot, peeled and grated
1 cup bean sprouts, coarsely chopped

24 medium round or square
    rice paper wrappers
    (approx. 16 cm diameter)
1 cucumber, cut into short
    match sticks
24 fresh mint leaves (or
    Vietnamese mint leaves)
sweet chilli sauce or soy
    sauce, for dipping

Cook the rice vermicelli according to packet instructions. Drain and set aside. Put the lemon juice, fish sauce, soy sauce and sugar into a large bowl and mix together until the sugar has dissolved. Roughly chop the vermicelli and add to the lemon mixture along with the chicken, carrot and bean sprouts. Mix until combined.

Put 1 rice paper wrapper into a bowl of hot water for 30 seconds, or until just soft. Lay the wrapper on a clean tea towel and place a heaped tablespoonful of filling mixture towards the bottom of the wrapper. Add a couple of cucumber matchsticks. Roll up halfway and fold in the sides. Place a mint leaf along the fold and roll tightly to secure the filling. Repeat with the remaining wrappers and filling.

Serve with sweet chilli sauce or soy sauce for dipping.

makes 24

Mini quiches

1 small brown onion, finely diced

2 rashers free-range bacon, finely diced

½ cup pouring cream

1 egg

½ teaspoon Dijon mustard

3 sheets frozen shortcrust pastry (24 cm × 24 cm), just thawed

½ cup grated cheddar cheese

12 cherry tomatoes, cut into three slices

Preheat the oven to 180°C (160°C fan). Sauté the onion and bacon in a small frying pan over medium heat for 5 minutes or until the onion is soft, but not brown. Transfer to a plate to cool.

In a small bowl, whisk together the cream, egg and mustard until well combined. Lay out the pastry on a chopping board. Cut out 36 rounds with a 5.5 cm pastry cutter. Gently press the rounds into three 12-hole (20 ml) mini non-stick muffin tins.

Sprinkle the onion and bacon into the pastry cases followed by 1 teaspoon of the cream mixture. Sprinkle with cheese and top with a slice of cherry tomato (cut side up).

Bake for 15 minutes or until golden and crisp.
Leave in the tins for 5 minutes before turning out.

makes 36

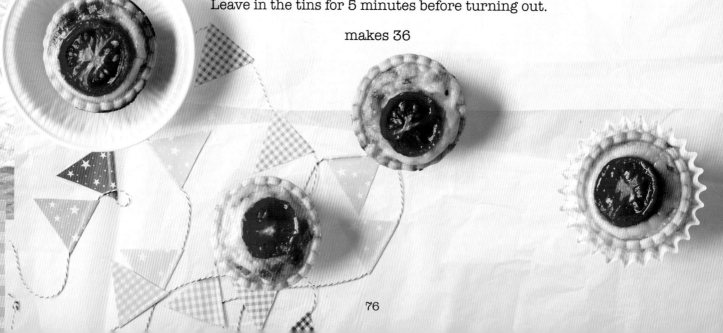

Banana split sundaes

8 small bananas, halved
1 litre ice cream (vanilla or
 another flavour of your choice)
coloured sprinkles, to serve

Peanut brittle
⅓ cup caster sugar
50 g salted roasted peanuts

Raspberry sauce
150 g frozen raspberries
2 tablespoons sugar

Fudgy chocolate sauce
150 g dark chocolate, chopped
½ cup thickened cream

To make the peanut brittle, line a small baking tray with baking paper and set aside. Place the sugar in a medium frying pan and cook over medium heat for 3–5 minutes, shaking occasionally, until the sugar caramelises. Add the peanuts, and use a fork to coat the nuts in the caramel. Spread onto the tray, and set aside to cool. Once cool, chop coarsely.

To make the raspberry sauce, place the frozen raspberries, sugar and 2 tablespoons of water in a microwave-safe bowl and microwave for 2–3 minutes, stirring occasionally, until the raspberries are soft and the sugar has dissolved. Set aside to cool, then process in a blender until smooth.

To make the fudgy chocolate sauce, place the chocolate and cream in a microwave-safe bowl. Microwave, uncovered, on medium power for 1–3 minutes, stirring occasionally with a metal spoon until smooth.

Place each banana in a dish and top with 2 scoops of ice cream, raspberry or chocolate sauce, peanut brittle and sprinkles.

Tip: if you like your chocolate sauce to set hard like the one in the photo, you can use the chocolate sauce recipe on page 63 instead.

makes 8

If you put the different toppings in bowls your guests can make their own sundaes just the way they like them. Fun!

Chef's chocolate cake

2 × quantities basic chocolate cake
  (see page 41)
100 g ready-to-roll white icing
small silver cachous, to decorate
large silver cachous, to decorate
14 mini marshmallows, cut in half

Chocolate cream cheese icing
100 g butter, softened
250 g cream cheese, softened
1 ¾ cups icing sugar, sifted
⅔ cup cocoa

Preheat the oven to 170°C (150°C fan). Grease and line two 20 cm round cake tins and line with baking paper.

Make the chocolate cake mixture and divide equally into the prepared tins. Bake for about 45–50 minutes or until a skewer inserted into the centre comes out clean. Leave in the tins for 10 minutes before transferring to a wire rack to cool. Trim the domed top off both cakes.

Place one of the cooled cakes on a plate or cake stand, trimmed side up, and spread half of the icing (see below) on top. Top with the second cake, trimmed side down, and spread the remaining icing on the top.

Roll out the white icing on a surface lightly dusted with icing sugar or cornflour (or between 2 sheets of baking paper) to 2–3 mm thickness. Using the picture as a guide, cut out a chef's hat shape with a sharp knife. Decorate the hat with small cachous and carefully place on top of the cake. Decorate the border of the cake with the large cachous and the marshmallow halves.

To make the icing: using an electric mixer, beat the butter and cream cheese until well combined and smooth. Add the icing sugar and cocoa, and beat until light and fluffy.

Conversion table

Weight

Metric	Imperial
10–15 g	½ oz
20 g	¾ oz
30 g	1 oz
40 g	1½ oz
50–60 g	2 oz
75 g	2½ oz
80 g	3 oz
100 g	3½ oz
125 g	4 oz
150 g	5 oz
175 g	6 oz
200 g	7 oz
225 g	8 oz
250 g	9 oz
275 g	10 oz
300 g	10½ oz
350 g	12 oz
400 g	14 oz
450 g	1 lb
500 g	1 lb 2 oz
600 g	1 lb 5 oz
650 g	1 lb 7 oz
750 g	1 lb 10 oz
900 g	2 lb
1 kg	2 lb 3 oz

Volume

Metric	Imperial
50–60 ml	2 fl oz
75 ml	2½ fl oz
100 ml	3½ fl oz
120 ml	4 fl oz
150 ml	5 fl oz
170 ml	6 fl oz
200 ml	7 fl oz
225 ml	8 fl oz
250 ml	8½ fl oz
300 ml	10 fl oz
400 ml	13 fl oz
500 ml	17 fl oz
600 ml	20 fl oz
750 ml	25 fl oz
1 litre	34 fl oz

Note: A pint in the US contains 16 fl oz; a pint in the UK contains 20 fl oz.

Cups

This book uses metric cup measurements, i.e. 250 ml for 1 cup; in the US a cup is 8 fl oz, just smaller, and American cooks should be generous in their cup measurements; in the UK a cup is 10 fl oz and British cooks should be scant with their cup measurements.

20 ml	1 tablespoon

Temperature

C°	F°
140	275
150	300
160	320
170	340
180	350
190	375
200	400
210	410
220	430

Length

Metric	Imperial
5 mm	¼ in
1 cm	½ in
2 cm	¾ in
2.5 cm	1 in
5 cm	2 in
7.5 cm	3 in
10 cm	4 in
15 cm	6 in
20 cm	8 in
30 cm	12 in

tail piece goes here

dinosaur
body template
Trace this template onto
baking paper and cut out.
Attach tail to body.

To make sure your
measuring is precise, try
weighing your ingredients!
1 cup flour = 150 g
1 cup caster sugar = 220 g
1 cup cocoa = 100 g

dinosaur
tail template